CALL STEPS

CALL STEPS

·

Plains, Camps, Stations, Consistories

KENNETH IRBY

Station Hill
_____
Tansy Press

Published by Station Hill Literary Editions under the Institute for Publishing Arts, Inc., Barrytown, New York 12507, in association with Tansy Press, Lawrence, Kansas with grateful acknowledgement to the National Endowment for the Arts, a federal agency in Washington, D.C., and the New York State Council on the Arts, for partial financial support of this project.

Title page drawing by Lee Chapman.

ACKNOWLEDGEMENT

Many of these pieces were first published (often in differing versions) by the following editors and publications: Robert Bertholf, *Credences*; Fred Buck, *Bezoar;* Paul McDonough, *Glitch*; Jed Rasula and Don Byrd, *Wch Way*; Mark Karlins, *Text*; Bradford Morrow and Nathaniel Tarn, *Conjunctions*; Nathaniel Mackey, *Hambone*; John Moritz, *Tansy*; Charles Bernstein, *Paris Review*; Jonathan Greene, *Truck*/Gnomon birthday collection for Jonathan Williams; Bruce McClelland, *Trumps*; Donald Powell, *Padma*; Richard Blevins and William D. Shields, Jr., *Zelot*. Three pieces also appeared as broadsides, printed by Jed Rasula in Los Angeles and by Tansy Press and by Helen in Lawrence, Kansas. Another was used on a poster prepared by Diane Hueter-Warner for the Lawrence Arts Center. An earlier version of OREXIS was published by Station Hill Press. To all those concerned, for their kindness, care, and encouragement, the author wishes to express his deep thanks, and as well to those responsible for the production of the present book, most especially Curtis Dillon, John Moritz, George Quasha, and Susan Quasha.

Library of Congress Cataloging-in-Publication Data

Irby, Kenneth, 1936-
   Call steps : plains, camps, stations, consistories / Kenneth Irby.
     p. cm.
   ISBN 0-88268-090-0
   I. Title.
   PS3559.R2C28 1992
   811'.54—dc20   91-3422
                                    CIP

in the life
in the work
for

Robert Grenier

shadow substance one
as is in the wind

Thomas Meyer

mind's flame dissolves
heart's icy sleeve

Gerrit Lansing

This *and* this *we say and do*
and so we fix each other up and this *is how transcendence is.*

.

Quae tibi, quae tali reddam pro carmine dona?

For such song, what gifts in return?

— Virgil
(tr. Stanley Lombardo)

TABLE OF CONTENTS

OREXIS   (1977)

Heredom

Running Lights

Erratics

CICADA WOODS   (1978)

The Winterground

Études

Strings

BOWLS (1979)

To return to this work now and offer it, a dozen and more years since its writing, is to reaffirm all its dedications (the *dēdicāre* and the *deik-* — the proclaiming and the justice: the pronouncing) and all its debts, formal and implicit, throughout — *in the life / in the work*, and to come.

*

What humility is there then in saying 'as best I know'? It is in an intoxication that I exclaim this. Speech rushes up from the bewilderd soul, out of knowledge, to claim its place in the vastest harmonies.

— Robert Duncan

What is not gathered is far more — perhaps the main thing.

— Walt Whitman

In vain we hope to be known by open and visible conservatories, when to be unknown was the means of their continuation and obscurity their protection.   .   .   .

To weep into stones are fables.

.   .

To live indeed is to be again our selves .   .   . Ready to be any thing, in the extasie of being ever

— Sir Thomas Browne

道　可　道　非　常　道

Lodehead lodehead-brooking : no forewonted lodehead

— Lao Tzu
(tr. Peter A. Boodberg)

[Lawrence, 1991]

CALL STEPS

Den Gåvan heter Avstånd
O du, som är stor i kärlek
du fanns där
och du gick tyst förbi

That Gift is called Distance
O you who are strong in love
you were there
and you passed quietly by

— Gunnar Ekelöf

OREXIS

Heredom

—

toute la vie terrestre procédant du feu est attirée par le feu qui réside au centre. Nous avions voulu qu'en retour le feu central fût attiré par la circonférence et rayonnât au dehors: cet échange de principes était la vie sans fin.

all terrestrial life originating in fire is attracted by the fire that dwells in the center. We had desired that in return the central fire would be attracted by the circumference and radiate without: this interchange of principles would be eternal life.

—Gérard de Nerval

lobe of opalescent glass
      broken in the irreplaceable lampshade

out of the shoulder, the corridor
      down the street the kids from junior high
          come by in t-shirts for the warmth of February
                                pigeons overhead
    stamp and cry in their sleep

gathered, the branch of acacia
      fused through the green swirled
          Egyptian thorn milk waters
raised, itself, of the lost and gathered body of mastery

or all the high school years again, unslept, reviewing the annual faces over and over
    till they run green in the movies after the eyes are closed
      and still as distant as they were in person

                the society of ordinary
          high school days, never left, will it?

         against the society of the widow's son, those
           who on the elephant's back
              be freed?

the generation of mourning doves' cries
    is from twilight in the mind
          releasing and attracting us

parsley

      pubic hair above the bread
         body torn to pieces and thrown at the audience

   or where the sun is gone
      or where we watch the empty place we were

claimed by the garden
   work to right again
      to grab the rock hair green
         up out of the dirt

grabbing against and to be in those rites
   whose body in the bed, whose car lights down the street
      through the monk's cloth curtains
         or by the corridor of the shoulder

      every bundle of the exultant stride of walking home

in the life of the laundry   the hand goes down
                                                                      into the patch

                        upside down the parsley hangs

                        and very very young the mothers are
                            one kid already 3 or 4
                            the one her mother calls "hey asshole"

                        we want to watch where each master *was*
                            the shape of the space left
                                just a curl of smoke behind
Aaron's cigarette in front of the brazen serpent, or some dope, or the cold in on the breath

                            in the same room

[for Mary Josephine Buffington Newman, 20 Jul 1884 - 20 Feb 1977]

in the well between our houses
        where the houses have gone to stare
        away from all their inhabitants

three violinists play your procession away
        under the pear tree, under the liriodendron
        under the ghost of the pear tree

the well of roses, the well of iris
        out back, down the alley
        down the ravine the waters carry away

   .

call of the Frisco diesel in the middle of the night

answering cry in the pigeons' sleep

waking not in a sweat but the smell of the sweat of waking

so far the call

even so the wavering fires

                        now just ordinary flameshaped lightbulbs set in a
                            triangle, purposefully crude and bare

            but as a child it was the unexperienced richness
                that made wonder

    in the palm of the youngest entered initiate
            without asking in the dark pupils watching, unseen

Light can be ordinary even when revealed and still by the spoken word
            astound the body least of all attended
                    out on the playground

                    I dropped the bag of groceries I didn't even mean to bring
                    I shit my pants *after* coming down from under the pine trees

        from the old authoritarian high degrees of Europe
            one aging man left to confer

    the camps, unattended, meant Westward

kept going on the decks, dark adepts at the flames

children of excitement
purses of the abandonment — not *yours* but *you*

     the Prince of the Captivity with a defective brain
     chased down the street by his father
          oblivio-naked to the usedto judgement of the kids looking on

the jewel hangs from a rattle string
     a broken rattle rayed with stars coming out from behind the occultation

and bars, like candy, out of prison

        sperm
            might as well have been hyacinth jizz or dandelion
        fuming on the palm

the man that might have been
master still and covered, to rise again

early Summer in SE Kansas
                    the second weekend in April, Good Friday, 85°

                broiled in bourbon before the Council of the Emperors of the East and West
                    hickory smoked in almonds, and the redbuds in glory, call

            and in the temple to be the temple substitute after the temple destroyed
                    and until

        not of Jerusalem yet of a secrecy within, of Jerusalem
            such election, which takes that history as its own
                    as ordinary and electable, rare, attended, as each tulip
                        each hyacinth passed, to each grape hyacinth, kinless, except

is still just beginning Spring

                        and in the temple, under the immense weight of tulips
                            the lights are extinguished
                                and the halls for the space of three days
                                    wait dark in the heart, cool

from The Camp the cries of burnt Templars
        rise into a canopy of transparent tintinnabulating leaves
            over the tents of the *tengu* and outward
                over the nonagon of the body, over the levees of patrol

you've probably caught sight of The Camp at times
            coming unexpectedly into a clearing and looking up
        the quick flags
              thinking a fairy ring of mushrooms
                or Kim's Red Bull on a Green Field

but it does not remain to the eyes
        or even, since there may be no other name, at all
and yet returns

it might have been having word of an old high school friend
        living in New Orleans now, grown large as his father
        that I circled Louisiana last night, marking only
            a couple of tents, or banners, or worn places in front in the grass
              named by the friends I knew were there

it is said as the troops move about The Camp and take up their positions with their speeches
                        taped to their spear shafts

        that the seven is empty

           so there is a space to look out on
              from the beasts and the heart and the ark between the
                        palms
           and into from the tents

           where the shade and choir of torment
              make an alleyway of repose to walk in
                from the work done, in the pause, on
              to the anticipation of the ball lying just out of hiding
                    around the bend
              and the shot clear to
                    but not to any hole in the hand
                    or the eye, waiting

The Camp if it is a camp rotates slowly on an axis
        not the Grand Commander or the Mill of the Heavens or the Transparency of the Tree
            or all the Years of Reunion Rituals
that are the pole of the body

. . .

across the street, in the next block North and East, next door to Howells' old place
next door to Jents' old place

a new van, chocolate brown and cream, parked out front, everybody standing around
looking at it

the Prince of the Captivity ran just there

Princess now, raced past me as I came back from Whiteside's last Thursday afternoon
her mother just after her, calling

so the word is passed on
and equally not known
till how much later, the thrill of recognizing can still be known

the iris guard young flesh, probably

Running Lights

— nun ists, als wäre mein Herz um Meilen hinausgeruckt, ich seh viele Dinge, die aufbrechen und die Richtung nehmen darauf zu —, aber ich erfahre nicht, daß sie ankommen.

— now it's as though my heart had moved miles away, I see many things that start and head off in its direction —, but I don't learn of their arriving.

—Rainer Maria Rilke

race of readiness before o'ertaken
Josephson's sungod's mirror's
I grown dark, I like waking
dark dots

rapt patience in the sun, not our lives
the *old* Grier drunk and raging
made as a warning
braineaters wait at the stone garage

a halohaired youth and return to youth
aloft in the breast of the *tengu*
come back «as halfwits
or as miraculous»

guardian of the lifted crystal thermos
instruments «of mountains, of huge trees»

sing with the taken

hard to believe just some shaved plain chocolate
all them days'd come back again, all of us saying we're the other one
                                    claiming to be the right one

cruising up and down between the dinner hour and the first picture show
                                    window shopping, arguing
hell I never known none a that love you said I took shit

earlier it was "Denmark", later it was old high Plateauro
long long after we was kids

right here's the river rind
after the corn

and on that road only a little time at the meeting to look around and see where we are as we talk

and smell the asshole smell of fucking mixed in with clover on very small dark hills and rain

and jars in the distance to fill again and then set straight and for that too only a little while

sometimes it's lying there in the mud at the start of the path
sometimes there's just a dent left in the dirt

you can hear the tennis balls thwack behind you as you look
the serious songs of summer end sung nervously and tight

big brown egg of a bear you can just smell the damp fur through
pale pink underfingernailfleshed smoothgrained egg of a flying pig
         more delicate and graceful than any wingèd creature

Frog Ben Webster, wet Kbhn, unsad persistence
as glory, gone, held on to, unlost

                                        «writing *that* kind of poetry»
«out of small irreducible sensual wholes»

            & I, by carnal hope
                    «without even listening to the inborn tendency to dominate»
            by cardinal home, an eye

in the wee small hours of the bed   enjoy the cold clear storm

                    vouchsafed, led

                                        unthunder, jewel

        all that *high old net*
                you'd just as soon slam into & forget
                            o'motions

                                    as easily the rain back

three streams in the Northern Kingdom
only the last left to cross

but the heart wants somewhere else
much as it just keeps on looking, pleased with the view, it won't cross

North, or you could call it straight ahead
                                        the coaxers calling
come on, come on over, use the spillway, just under the flow, it's ok
                                                        hands out

but no, not yet

turn West instead, down to the street where the big fur slot machine taller than a man's head
figures return up out of the blankets spread out to sell

and in the South two inns, a night club and a diner, side by side
too early to be open except to sudden friendship in the dark
hard to get any sandwich parasols, any sandwiches, even
and then set out for the giant cottonwoods on the Northeast heights

I don't know the East

it's as much to say it's all a flag

                        geranium crown above the walrus ivory king
                            upon a green baize ground
                        flattened across the palm of the *jism*

but even granting allegience to the clarity, the days of true experience, the whole life there

                the heart yearns another cause

38

      's

bear'shead slot   congruent with   watches' lamppost showrack

      on the street

    to renew at a time of the dump of cities

          meeting

«carried as one room of air around us»   a rite out of 18th century
I thought when I wrote that was component   rot of privilege
  of an opened Western shore
    still possible to discover new   suppressed city
        Point Reyeses

      heart, too, of revolution

baculus virtual   where «air» = pneuma
      virgin branched   from each to each   off the top of the head
    verga flowered *cojones*

        and the feet share
wire rite   gladly given will
    radiate

    «men loveable men»

  «inviolable in their promises»

blood in the clouds means   whatever all the failed shots with the rifle
fail

"just your big career of interruptions"

whose *jism*
it was *to get it back* took aim

from squirrels, or people so far off they're small as squirrels, flicked tails, quick as
squirrels
and be filled

and later on the song the other side they sang so sad
the heart took heart, the rooms it carried
into one with
squirrel and rabbit, crow and duck and toad and mole
home stomping in the mud

morning   "sparks 18 feet long off the grapevine"   *news?*

                    doubled under me to eat

                                        tents raised and struck
                                        all night long across the bed

to "heaven's radio, on the other shore"

                    autumn calls travel — K-F-A-L
                         -ken
                    that oa-   to-   flute of leaves
                         -ten

the ball game of the continent
     «Captain, fishpainter»
          high up on the wall

                                   writing with a ballpoint hardon

               whirling, sparkling

                              transparent as an asshole

          tip it is

«and so those values once masked by shock enter into the judgement of a later
                    generation»

«it never *even* entered my mind»

                    all this time, the filagree again
                    the ceiling lace of virgin acid

                    nasturtium, geranium, hyacinth
                    tilth of grass

or had so slight a song to go on had to fuck it up

                         the up returns

      and *thy* redemption to say *even*

                    «partaken of the banquet to which
                    the invited guests did not come»

[variation on *L'homme armé*, i.e.: «o the man, the man, the man of arms
                    he fills the folk with dread alarms» etc.]

passed a lean tall man in the woods with a big dark eye
dark as cars in a sleet storm, hooked and dry

looked for him to show up later in the library john or up using the copy machine by the book
                                                    return
glaring people away

wouldn't want him here telling stories when the snow storm cut us off
but Lordamercy find out, what's he *say*

cold water and mud, clear to the bone
worry you straight on out of your home
                    permanent

[towards an homage to John Dunstable]

& my my tongue waggle with the like power to share the roads
and in the tavern with the dogs
share the fading away of the voice from the heights
as the mass made
sung off

as winter comes on
our fate to have the coldest moon born in us

& turn wanting to know the other man
fast as the hand'd ever move, there
the emptiness of life its gate, left far behind
the knob slid down the bar, without a word

the West lit, the laundry gone, thereby the call

great ring year, horse rolling on its back, feet up in the air
now this way now that, on the finger in the depth of the eye
and step forth into the goatfish ocean, cold churning at the balls

talk to me, but I won't answer
only smile, stoned stranger at the party, on the sofa in the corner
roseweave throw over the shoulders and the silver lamp lit

comes the speaker soon, whose staff like a camp lifts
and gives liege to the stones that exalt the breath

& if the face is pale

now mercy is the gone
upon our snow

Erratics

Et comme un oeil naissant couvert par ses paupières
Un pur esprit s'accroît sous l'écorce des pierres!

And like a nascent eye covered by its lids
A pure spirit grows beneath the skin of stones.

— Gérard de Nerval
(tr. Robert Duncan)

Kanske Gudinnan av hyn
· · ·
i blanka vårdar

Perhaps the Goddess of skin
· · ·
in the polished headstones

— Harry Martinson

[overheard]

— you get any more calls back here than you did just thinking about being back here?

— it's probably got more to do with wherever who's asking, I mean it's more a place in me than all these people I don't know?

— like Lehnhoff's wanting to take you out to dinner?

— and all those "family" boarders waiting at home to deal with first, a lot worse than any momma or poppa to get out past — who says Lehnhoff's Lehnhoff?

— who is it then, Big Daddy?

— why, because he asked me out to eat, and it's all in just the first letter of each word?

— yeah, and it's a ritual — cipher, monitor, and that they were *given* to you — now, while you're still alive, to lead you out

— no no no no, it's like all the same *there*, nobody's *after* me here any more than, actually *less* than I'm after *them* — and anyway, it can't just be age or poppa or filthy blue deer, or I mean blue boarders, or big blue balls, or who's dead and who isn't, but *every*body, and *really*, the question is how we ever get *back*

— "bring me an orange soda, with a little order of hot sauce on the side" — you got out sliding down a pole outside your bedroom window when you were 5

— no, that *was in*, I got *out* by realizing it was just a dream and I wasn't going to hit the bottom— right where the redbud is, just exactly where that redbud is now

— you think the pigeons're making room for you every night stamping and moaning and carrying on up there?

— more than likely, they've brought the plaster down on me twice already and probably will again

— but look, that's not it, is it, we're losing track, it's the call, and the call is too, is just like you said it was, only you were asking for it, you were praying for it—*only pay attention once again*

[Heredom]

my farewells of vacancy of mind

        later I'll come back to what's been kept there

        but the sad corners of rooms, up near the ceilings
        that will not ever return

my own lost skin
that will not be redeemed by another inhabitant, nor redeem, nor haunt

        but meet again, not turned away
        out of the glory of the woodwork

[«the Heron of Oblivion»]

the mirror at the culmination of the old degree
beyond the staircase, after the lecture of each step's toppled columns reerected
in the dark then, afterwards, alone in the closet beyond them
left to meditate on the iron ring's death head first seen and now again, the blood rust

                                        at the culmination of the 2d of the old rite
                                        at the top of the stairs in the sudden light
                                        instead of the expected guide
                                        the candidate, yourself, in a mirror

*

so Robert Duncan's propositions of the mirror in *The Venice Poem*:

        "Imaginary Instructions":   1:   «in the poem as mirror — the whole world,
                                                      an instruction.»

                                      2:                              «in the mirror
                                              the Part —
                                              consternation of a whole world.»

                                      3:      «a realistic image
                                                      as if that virgin upon St. Agnes Eve
                                                      had seen
                                                      old Nobody
                                              wearing a face in the mirror.»

                                      4:      «the mirror as imitation, as poem»

        «Yet here seeks the heart solace.»

                                        «seeing already
                                          more than Love's mirror shows»

                «as if only here,
                here it might rest»

I met the Angel Sus on the Skin Bridge
the Bridge Chinvat, offertory
my image crossing the basketball court and taking the path into the woods
and at the other end, in the gravel at the bend of Terrace Road
more expressive than the small red heart-shaped lips of the Lizard Mother, your endlessly
    mobile face
snout cloud of light and bristles thicket of impenetrable brightness
and smile of infinite frenzied utter patience
nostrils as close to my brow as opened clover
only a face! only a face! only a face!
wings but the knot clod sfumato uncertain noose clothing
over the skin we share, organ me you share
was it John telling me to turn to you, in crowded Houlihan's on the Plaza, with Charlie and the
    bears in the dark
brought me to you, you came out this far to meet me
where the VW's been parked since at least last March and the horses' empty field comes in
    close and the houses begin
"You must make me the Clean Compound
first, before you pass through me"
each to each?

slowly the old stone building walls downtown dissolve
dropped in the pond of wind in the August noon
slow slow motion salt castles by the time the stoplight changes at 7th and New Hampshire
from the eyes the old world goes, across the river the cables of resistant skin, tight enough to
    walk on

the young who work to bare the body soft again as the crown of geranium petals fallen
no heaven that might redeem the past but only make way over and over again for the protection
    flowers give to age at all
to what it hasn't yet accumulated, most of all

the speed that ungoos the eyes is some reward, certainly, out of the South with the wind
as age comes up out of the ground polar as the brain lode at the same time as it goes back
    down in under the feet again

homegrown handtipped dervishwhirling in your own living room without getting dizzy or sick,
    taught by somebody in the speech department who goes to Naropa every summer
where such things usually accumulate, at the end of August, not an early time at all, but late
    as fatherhood
Excelsior as the tight foreskin of what desire's called o'er-reaching that never knows its own
    phone number
and continues at the mercy of, at the mercy of, at the mercy of
savage as the «endless rumination of the Big Vegetarians» wasping the lateral world of vision
    to the narrow waist of instant jumpup Whizz
and over all of it not even a guardian moth or a gnat but probably just the flick of a pig with
    wings, quicker than jizz sop

[homage to Andrei Bely — *the memory of the memory of speech*]

so came to old friends' shapes and voices playing soul

host theophanic *caro mio spiritualis*

lost deference before the images of power nor gained

every association with who seem to be

whole coat loan the rite of purge transition

ache of *the street rooms* on the road home *parts of the body*

dealing presence equal to subsistence shared

work by the phone booth hand plates yearn for meat

cheap change the text books ritz construe

and all the me's the means to bridge -ceptivity made clear

the paths of ancient initiation are

[two postcard views — homage to the Gérôme and Van Gogh-Hiroshige Kriophoros]

from Timotha and Gerrit and Shannon

Hermes Ram-Toter enters the snow-filled clearing just after the duel has ended, the young fool in the Pierrot costume dying, the Hiawatha fullback slickster stumbling away with his second, stunned and mumbling — by the time they get to their car nothing will be visible but the mindbuggering freezing fog — and Herm Sheep-Finder comes up to the Pierrot and takes him out of the arms of his death-glazed friends, hoists him over his right shoulder and walks on off into the woods, the masquerade costume falling away leaving the body naked — between death and the ram, kouros-lean, that passes understanding

*

the land and the sea that keep the bridge arched level slant violently upward to the left, that Northwest, or Home Against Fall, as the view from aloft banks to the right for the limitless ocean — and to cross the bridge goes on out of sight into the rain, probably even curves back again somewhere further on this same shore — three go crossing, three coming back, bent under the drench, wet fleece under one arm, wet belly and flank against the neck, phallos hat, wingless, who can see Fortune curving migratory as the continents, bullet-out and -back

[given: three beavers in a tree]

by their long hair, as now my own a few gray strands joins
call the color age, or of the work'd, silver
above the waters?   later the tree came into the living room and took on golden balls and
    butterflies
psyche'd opening   above the still-opening crown bud gold sun clearing the gold horizon
14 points of light   perfect elect, sublime   24 globes of month roads
preening their whiskers along the soft short needle spines
back into the   almost said and let stand for all *the other*, forest
but not trees either   sandy tracks into, hearing the ocean, might be
rocks clashing   still with the glacier energy unreleased roar surf
against the hills   their whiskers more silver than their hair that joins us
eyes, liquid, aloft

something like such wilderness as interstates tie
without a comb's at all dimension   look, you can't *join* us, *be* us
all your yearning of another body   keeps you going
up against *we see you*   where the splendor'd crown bud bursts over and over
we'll give you a ride in our *brand new automobile*
even let you be our *handsome driver at the wheel*
even the Boy Scouts know that, honor our award
so, slowly, secretly, we come back up the Smoky Hill, the Republican
the big *big* cars, in among the stars
where you see bonechina butterflies in and out among the golden balls

sweet heavy load to carry   you think of as despair to ever *say*
the *saylessness*, the *talk to me* that does not talk, months on end
truck load after truck load
castoreum honey in the graven shell
old base glory!   we gnaw down to tell

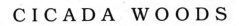

CICADA WOODS

Цитата не есть выписка. Цитата есть цикада.

A quotation is not an excerpt. A quotation is a cicada.

— Osip Mandelstam

The Winterground

The Body in winter is the hunting lodge

— Edward Dorn

[rocks]

I

slowly melts the old composure
whodya *want*? whoya *after*?

      love and travel, love and exploration
      love and all that old net of sweet association
      and only the outcry *at* is known, can't see back past or on
      desperate for the wet smell, for the water love

all this in the life of the area driving around town all night to get laid or get drunk or get high
   or *get*

      walked into behind Hoch coming home from the library this
        afternoon and thought it was the night before last out from
        under what? *crown*? and into the open
      came to starting up the stairs in the music library

      you were there

wherever, not the music library, no
where I've always found you
facing you scared, shy, heart high
no matter I've known you already forever

65

II

and not as Lance Kerwin said in *James at 15* tonight, love's only truly love if it's shared, taken
      and returned
but that it changes then, makes *us* a difference

                                                            unrequited vast histories of 15!
                                                            28, 41!
                                                            12, to get rid of and still encourage
                                                                keep at it and you'll, *some-
                                                                body'll*

pissing in the dark, hearing the voices from the living room

      .

distance? all that old distance to play all over again?

not over and not taken and not returned and not bearable *up close*, assuaged with red Korean
      wool and Atget?   taking *them*?

dear   —the hoquet—   *how*   *are you*   *there?*
      never enough   to live with   not even   to sleep with

      care?
   . . .   but *distance*

when we lived in the same town one month you threw me a birthday party the next not even an
      invite to your New Year's Eve
but all *sorts* of kindnesses and generosity

deep, *unbearable* affection?   except for *distance*

wearing the new red shirt you sent   rubs off on my underwear

III

the distance, the distance love
the through, the active through

and the middle voice
to see through oneself
where the verb is the you
and the self is the both of us
and the watcher is the I
and the distance the love, active through

but *to stand apart*

how close you are, how easily
I forget you, impossible
passing you, coming back

[for Jack Howell – 1]

we made the world together
as *grass*, and *bones*, and *thanks*

like the Frisco, and death, and Westerns
roulette on an upturned wagon wheel

cast like taking on the telephone for life
to call the stars

[for Jack Howell – 2]

there is a man in both of us
when we meet in dreams *others, others* is

and memory is oblique preparing for
being unprepared where

nowhere else can matter

hear my slow brother me
hearing me hearing all
tongue Thoth's turned from
ears bent over the table, cluttered

share increasingly
ineptitudes together
kindly even as to never
how many we are

how many of us got in the car last night
carrying Jack Howell's long dead dad too drunk to stand
out of trouble and took off?
and though the me at the wheel, the car drove us

all I of the family, how different from each other we are
not even in dreams do we know each other's dreams
or that we dream
the others call?

the distance of love is one of the cracks in the year
help through, like smoke, like last night
wet the soul but not love the possible death
smelling like chase when the fever's irresistible
and get it right

[homage to Kasimierz Przerwa-Tetmajer (2 Dec 1865 - 18 Jan 1940)]

to be claimed in the end by the fate of some old poem
dying *its* life

the unprotected sop of experience for size
hot
shit!
hotter, for having been off on its own for 30, 40 years
come home

Fern the waitress and *the parking meters of July*
racing the melos to the final gasp

and go out tracking the wheel down the gutter muttering
something I forgot I wrote I forgot

for always talking home
the end is sure to be without
the soul, too level
wants to go *its*
down
and out

but *up one flight of stairs I long to climb*

and so *its* life *to go*
still slips which mine?

[a Valentine for Tom Meyer's birthday]

she would want to call me, far far indirection to my unready ears, to reach me,
only if I wondered, *who* beyond *who* I heard, for all of us

                                      "what about those
heart's hands you whacked, uh, walked off with" — clear as the stoplight, and
no more — "you gone run over, that's un*full*filled"

                                           strength to hear whatever
voices speak the truth to you, as part of you, all up *till then, and on* — you really
think that place you *got* matters, instead of what you got to *make*, right now, *on?*
it's made, no matters

                          she'd want to, only when I turned away and wondered,
who said that to who said that, by heart

                                    made, no matters — but do I ever
really believe that, ever know it's done for sure, till afterwards? staring into the
future as if that were *ahead*, when she says, she says *who* to *who* she says, *my
word exalts, nemmine*

late in the Winter when thaws beginning Spring should long ago have started, the cold persists, no more heavy snows but frozen mists, thin sleets, leftover snow grimy, brooding the woods, the yards, the trash in upper rooms waiting for brighter, warmer days to be taken out, bent over above the porches, waiting, for footsteps soon to come, and talk, up there

I used to go up in the late afternoons, not long before sunset, and sit in the bare attic, looking out West and North, toward the river, the hills on the other side of the flood plain brighter than anything else in the day, snowdark the woods — and watch till the aftersunset glow had vanished and the room was dark, the earth turn

the space of time in a life between a year of waking and a year of sleeping, to wake again, and then go downstairs, turn on the lamps in the living room, put on some music out of the shadows, make a drink, start fixing dinner — and the life too would come into the room, out of the burrow of earth under the snow in the woods, like the figure of a dog molded in snow in the woods, shake, and rouse itself, and come in

how useless insistence *want*
when *heart* is *face* the *dream* itself entirely makes
share circling the shore
desire generation *attain* to exaltation, not possession
reed-girt, sun suddenly falls on

great wonder that we ever *saw* each other
or the face made not of yours and mine but all the crossing in
we still find, still look into

stirring chicken wings, staring out the kitchen window over a clear, old city
wings, those vanished communes long ago melted quiet down the farms to pits, stirring gathers
    in your eyes again, gin and ginger, lemon and soy, sweet hotcha ever name again

or pyracantha massed along the fence in back, how long to see back into that dark corner of
    the yard, watching the oven door, checking the brownies bake

skipping rocks out to sea
too bright to look at
at to face

then pointed to the opposite hills, your true homeland, who carry, you, or you, them, unvisited, that oldest home, the buried sea, and hearing's ground, now here, and *now's* a few hundred thousand years or just this, now moved on, another ice, another job, another long haul, rocks piled up in hubs and spokes and rims to get back to the sky again, singing, shouting, stamping time, following the route signs up and down, up and down, *straight up*, like breathing, round and round and round and round, till that reach unsufferable return

*

two young runners cut the town from North to South, always brothers, always a pair, one with the pipe, one with the power stick held out in front, and ever on the distant horizon the redshouldered hawkheaded hounddog, in a big black Stetson, with the Sun Dance scars above each tit, turns his profile back and forth, back and forth, singing: *getting it on, getting it on, you always gotta keep getting it on*, then jeering, taunting, goading: *yahhh, leave it to me, leave it to me, sure, all you can do is leave it to me — come on, thread me, thread me, thread me, thread it on through me*

*

but it was still my fault we got lost, and when we finally did make it on to the next family visit, they kept asking, but what do yall *do*? o God, I said, I've tried *every*thing, and never any luck — if I could fry cook fast enough I'd run for Burger King — o yes, she said, and what about the new place I keep hearing about, Prayer Burger? haven't the heating bills just been awful this winter?

over the cliffs it has to be, and toss this martial earth aloft, to empty out the hard-held heart and hands and reach, o brother clouds, your house above the sea, o sister earth, o sister sea

Études

Brer Fox, he come up, en der lay Brer Rabbit, periently cole en stiff. Brer Fox he look at Brer Rabbit, en he sorter *study*.

— Uncle Remus

Die Sprache der Natur ist einer geheimen Losung zu vergleichen, die jeder Posten dem nächsten in seiner eigenen Sprache weitergibt, der Inhalt der Losung aber ist die Sprache des Postens selbst.

The language of Nature can be compared to a secret password that each sentry passes on to the next in his own language, but the meaning of the password is the sentry's language itself.

— Walter Benjamin

attractions, steady
old affections, renewed
as if forgotten
energy, memory
celebration, being able to
to say

even that there
is someone there

dis   not of
tance   but from

some center love
from time to time

we feel each other
cross

time cold or
not to
trim the shag
lift the head
lightened to hear
the touch of
bear
the breath of
closening wings

documents enter Winter *read*
bright lead carved dull
life *occult* strained steps
seed old shoes tracks
new graven brain sing
even old memoried *eye*
clean one time more

the candle lit to
cast
the shadow tell to

tell the samba grown
celebrant, shadow
out of tune

made out of distance
what it claims it to
stand apart

make out of builders a crown
climax coffee on a door
face grave houndom into human hone

silver vessels in the bed
keep life of all the anger
making love
what string unlost
run through the pubic hair
surer than plastic
wrapping focus

steps of the camp
mud element of trance
essence star of hippopotamus
walking the bottom of the river milk

love left than a
weight lift then a
laugh less than a
way

love last then a wait
less than a left
laugh weigh than a lift

love left than a weight
lift less than a
laugh last then
away

[2 variations by Bob Grenier]

love left of a
weight less than a
laugh lift of a
way

love lift of a
weight less than a
laugh left of the
day

call snown draw   cold moon sawm

comb new leaver lean

so shadows dough

back into the darkening foliage trunks have gone
a man maybe takes sudden motionless
watching the swimmers past

cross to her
than knowing her

but the swirl
the sand under

smaller than almonds
bigger than peanuts
tears than hail
ground jaybirds bare

headed for the swimming pool
poorer than ever, maybe
but not without, though

kids go and throw towels
are but us

ever *who* on the way
like a tree holds, shows, from

brood(s) the woods
rear(s) the sun
warm(s) the ball
gone(s) the grass

angelical
fucking
unexpected things
out of
ask it, not jizz it

make a heart out of

arca the shape of

reach to the pell
etudes peloria

hunger the shavanon
exports the calm to

but   orexis   eagerness   apprehension   study

no one cares
unless the world is *really* changed
otherwise, *shoo*
but we *bay*-rasst, er ah, we *lost*-uss

gone to a quiet that hurts the toes

once the hypnotist never knew was blue

who thought a coast to glory?

[homage to Sōtatsu's *Bugaku*]

O I, left, right
red cloth, green
SW to or N to, W
mouthharp back or just flutes

O top I, both sides
door or rows

over or call the wet up seen
o tree right *o animal* left
ode all the uprights O'd
outsprung, unbōwed

& ear lobe told
just hold to be
or sway to weight
just tuss

or a man carries a pot in near noon
turn stone, but he, uh, don't see no sun in it
and the watcher, just kicks from habit

like a rock cast in the sea
hard, and gone, long gone

& so'd see into the undersun   though grinder

& trace a road where over again   low hold against thresh

note *Urdu* means *camp* (Turki)

where wasps over cottonwoods
quit ashes ashes ground

sadness   a wonder
        what is *full*

                             sæd   *sæd*   *sæd*   pebbles   -ted

     aid thirst weary filling

                                     to room?
                                     -tiness?

so make me sad not of my own

          *un*satisfied, o'erflown

                              'd

          dinosaur browse
          the secret sentence disappearance
          blood
          hot to the hand

one black currant seed in the teeth hole
another cricket by the *recencies*
between the leap
like petiole

trees pass
bees press
clouds talk

hair calls
how long damp
cottonwood

study is the gate of justice
in the doorway hammered zeal fingers the scales
three drops at a time, three more, forming
just sun of blood

between what is seen (heard)
and what is seen (heard)
what is   (   )
otherwise

or didn't never so much pay attention to as change back and forth with, someplace else

dark urchin sun
stretched heart yoga
yoke between leaves

cottonwood lingerers
still green
tops
still golden
boys

another life, high
and with the roots of stones

[requiem études · for Louis Zukofsky]

word   boundaries   orenda
                     sumbur
                     «If they ask, it is you»

                .

exalted   master
          asper
macbenac ma che ben' art' mackerinact
for 'im 'at's gawn awa'

                .

o Swan over the dark stripes
where light
bright oil
                     «To glow — not to grovel»

                .

from *It Was*   «"the country of Watteau"»
where everyone is just about to rise and go

light leaves like
black under wind

back of pagoya
& I-light, I-lid, I-through, back

                .

take light & dark
up the heart
                     «For the living»

Strings

for Ruth and Tad Palmer

David con unas tijeras
cortó las cuerdas del arpa.

David with some scissors
cut the strings of his harp.

— Federico García Lorca

[homage to Carolan]

or whether those words I'll never never be used by
or whether living with you those you's I never wrote to always apart, by

.

they took down the poles for volleyball from beside the swimming pool tonight put up just for
    the party this afternoon
as the wine bottles and newspapers gone by with to dump leave smudges to

.

long ago gave up home by the pole to

so how? by the in stant

and yet sweet distance by the love full

.

even the eyes their goo to
even the hands their come and gone to

even the swept far far away from

.

each other distance, each ours
as difficult by reference as by not knowing

each time, each name

.

even the match stroke smell left long long after now
the hair as fine as children shared

.

and all by being in the world incompetent
to pay for a life by earning

.

so take to bed the study of the child
and in that well the cry and bucket of the cry

.

a nightmare of *the man*, and another and another
and find the child, to raise, who but us?

.

and almost hear the hair the bone cannot
and never easily, but how willingly, to join

[for Charles Filiger's *Breton Cowherd*]

it might be Tad, the way he stands, the same age, 14, 15, but he'd probably have on clogs, not sabots anyway, and not an upsidedown sailor cap with a striped band, but the same faded blue denims, very well filled, head to one side, hand on hip, looking straight back just barely tolerant between boredom and devilment, the instant of pure outward introspective receptivity, like a saint

might be early spring, probably actually summer, but, early spring, the first buds on the bare branches, cowless

.

so we will cross the fields' stripes
as the Swan crosses the first, last, darkest river

not to come back, certainly
but together?

.

and the image of the boy, the image of the young man, the image of the man
between us, gone on his way, through us

.

a young man's call and acquiescence from the bank
his middle age lamenting, still above, brought back again from entering

now a wanderer, then a wanderer, over the fields' stripes

[embarras de]

& would it be body to
make *zealous liberality* a gift that's taken from

& if & if & if
        so smart

o why o why o why
        aintcha

[homage to Johannes Bobrowski]

or other dark days, in front of the first entering initiate's quavering in front of first entering, unshowing — walk up to that door in the heart, too, dark even in the morning, the morning spider not gone home at evening but not working across in front, only looking on

or ever work back through the crowds to the first seat high high up in the auditorium, still claimed with a bowler and a coat? fences fields and viaducts that way — or find the lost yellow robe, not for the robe itself, even though it still keeps the shape of right use and long wear, but for the message in the pocket — for this have we spoken with each encountered, of his poetry and in praise, to one, of the broadcast equipment, and the crowd at the door, to another, and mistaken clothing in the seats, and the path across the pasture — all this before everything gets started

a postcard of the Great Mosque, from Córdoba — Mt. Shasta at first light, from Oregon — two men bargaining for a horse, one of them just minding his whittling, from Cape Ann — a line of petroglyphs of riders on a canyon wall in Arizona, from Gallup — over all these, the Knight of the Sun, who is a Lion in Radiance but starting to turn away, starting to look on off over our right shoulders, slowly

once again brought before the first door at mid-September, the litter of just-yellowing leaves blown up against the threshold, shifting dark and light working underneath and gone, and the glitter of cottonwoods far off at the edges of the room, almost beyond the corners of the eyes

a door, and a dog that recognizes someone else and goes on into the room behind, and a sower, already for next spring, casting grass seed, in the shifting light, under broken clouds — knock 3 and 3 and 3, and each knock a drop hanging perfectly still in the air in front of the wooden panels

a boy there preparing to be a man in his mind reaches down into his pants and rearranges his cock in his shorts, takes his hand out and pulls his underwear down in back through the seat of his pants, walking on straddle-legged — noon time, still no rain, still some sun

perfectly still the widened shoulders at the corner, just the t-shirted back visible — in front of the door, he sees himself grown, in front of a woman, say, or steps down a hillside, and turn out of sight, and wasps circling there in the sun

and says to himself, *I trust the language of those who forget*

dark warm day, what a door that is to walk out through, come down out of the North during the night

you thought you could hear them singing, the wires in front of the woods, the crunch of gravel in the drive

I could see you going down the front steps past the tobacco bush and on out back to your bus, head down, listening

the wind up the canyon, the storm through the oak grove and the doves and the great basins of water, the tide clatter up the beach, the rain on the bay leaves, fingernails scratching the scalp

and saw you look into the surface of earth, the dark bowl coming up to meet the search

blowing their skirts just through on the other side, who walk with Fall down out of the North, dark and warm

and could hear you saying yes and yes and yes in your sleep, and smoothed along the curve below your breast, listening

what can trust take and wish were mine were yours
foolish most to only want to give to love

restless, the rain returns, the bergamot smell faint on the fingers yesterday from the Guerlain *Impériale* after shaving, today in the word, looking in vain for any certain or satisfactory etymology — smelling the *4711* lingering from following the curve of your throat and shoulders with my fingers — about now you'd be having dinner in some corner of Greece, the glass of cold water with the coffee afterwards, and maybe the cafe proprietor wanting to introduce Italian ways serves the coffee with a twist of lemon, the fine citrus oil shimmering on the surface, filling the nose as the cup is lifted — bent over the well into the dark depths, over the smooth-worn honey-colored marble rim, looking after where the stone has dropped, seeing nothing but the dark, hearing nothing after the rock splash but the trees, only the faint lemony bergamot-oil-in-cologne smell, dry as September, still suddenly abroad and gone — the face of us between us in the dark look close at who lies next to you taking away the twitching of the candle muscles in the thigh

so close to the wall the twitching does go by morning

lamb of the graven heart, look close at who passes through you, your sight illumination to

for those who in the dark reach through the thin almost impermeable membrance

[equinox variations - «by the sills of the exquisite flexible doors»]

petunia midnight purple throat
a life to share, more than, lit by, ever
crushed tomato vines ahead, burr of stramonium, hands unburying potatoes
kisses of capsicum, nic fits conquered, come and gone
the way out past what isn't ever guessed for
like
dependence
eggplant star eyes
Solanaceae heart glow

*

grass · well · piano keys : not glass or mirror scryed
but yoke · yoga : shouldered dark and light

*

leaning over, staring into the grass, into the piano player bending over the keys playing into
the Limbus

not to see anything but squarely take the yoke of light and dark

chrysanthemum, petunia, cottonwood hold out and in, such yoga the clear voice tells is
numbering

adding up your breathing in the dark against my back, the blades of grass, the shadows of the
blades of grass

[homage to the Dodonaean Rilke]

the cold calls travel — with the gone? with no *one*, maybe a many — *bundles, restless* — some
work no hand to, but *having*, harden the heart to those who don't — all understandable, core,
even, of what we think of as *union* now — not any longer the *nation*, or the *North*, though no
matter here, in the question of: *protection* — even the craft, true — what brotherhood of travel,
but death — *no way to know, but go back on to*

one reticence against another engenders sadness — and the excess, is *resented*? then regretted —
but no more revealed than not

.

servant of the bowl, the wind directs the beater
who *tells* the racket means?
    sadness requisite? that fullness
    to overflow to oracle

«Absents within the Line Conspire, and *Sense*
Things distant doth unite»

.

«Sure, there's a Tye of Bodyes!»

— *Silex Scintillans*, I

fog dreams, drop dreams, the fear of falling, singing, "Please help me, I'm falling" — and if the soul's natural movement is ever downward, deeper, what *fears*? we say we *fall* in love — the precipice of ruthlessness, the *love*? rather than *to, into, onto* some thing?

fog, and the cottonwoods do not glitter, though you can see them tremble — thins out over the woods, blown, then thickens again, and the cottonwood sapling by the tennis court stands for a moment clear against it, and the trembling very clear — but only in the heart the glitter

might be an egg, or a lemon, gone on down the rapids — rays break out of back at those on the bank receiving — hand by the blood flowing, up to the tree with the bark scraped — not just one way, the share, the tree takes on the disease, but the hand crashes with the timber, or the eye peeled with the egg, or the zest oil — bobbing, in white water

whether at fault
quaver at crack

the heart breaks
not the affections

each time
        winds oracle the body
                    it hurts

nothing helps that does not help
the passing day pass free

to die
out through

well who the hell can I have here
from the surface of each sphere a fine mist joins each sphere, the grass grows out of
there is a set of wrath pits in the earth such force comes out of that seeks sun building
back into the iridescent bubbles when it rains

ahhh go to hell and stay there
yeah every blade of grass's got to be stared at and ridden sitting up all night on the bus can't
    sleep
God, I'm *sorry* I got pissed off, how can I live like that?
grass and rocks and dumb regret lead to the water's edge, turn around and look back at the
    laundromat lodge, pays for getting clean

anger is focus, regret such mist, each drop

could transubstantiate the sudden terrible paternity of wrath
to the sudden terrifying joyful prodigality of love?

could ever love that way?

sweet iridescence of the pits?

[Winter saeta]

do you know the wound of the shoulder, hidden, that numbs the thumb, to ever let it go?

the keep of the bourbon that unlocks the spine keys, the little girl of the combs, secret arrow,
    far far up over the street, balcony finder, something good on tv nobody else can find out's
    going to be on?

                        she, too, counts leaves, singing
transfixes the apricot sunset, leaving season, you can taste

corn, and beans, makes the wind, chili, and tomatoes, colors no animal system lately — and none ever expected — but circling the flagstone steps then trap door to the underground where Pratt was, and I knew would be — uncle, connection — guide? — going down with and taking with, the young blond girl, yet knew, too — girl-Ruth, little-girl-Ruth, but grown, too, and not Ruth (never looked like), but also her — hardon Hermes came down out of the North and through Samothrace the mysteries there told why of, Herodotus said — Hermes Stiff-prick, Hermes Steel-dong and Smile-face, head-only (but with his dick out — handless — you bring me off, I you, but not ourselves) — square-in-ground — pink Sioux quartzite balls out of Minnesota, tough granular testicles out of the North, in the Kaw plain loam scrotum — set up around out in front of houses — Erratics-wayfinder, Erratics-lidless-painless, Erratics-lead-off — but to become lid-open and pool-open, who came here over and under, before and after, river-easy-ways — now stationary, -heart stone? step by step into that other-ground by all-around-town stepping on? — going under with, Ruth, being-little, both, sharing sexy-yet-to-be-for, together, needing, kindly as the uncle ever would be, -stone, -off?

[— and to Artemis]

so slight a lift, it seemed, the other night talking to you, because I couldn't think of what to say, going on about botfly larvae peeking out of wounds, but each night since, and in the day odd times, the towers rise, the resonance of your voice comes back in the stones' slight vibration, moss in the cracks like the insistent distant electric-clock hum of traffic on the freeway through the hand, or the pie baking and the pecans settling slightly, opening to the chess thickening underneath, lifting —

O Goddess of the Airways, who hear, over whose fine drawn hair the words string the continents and through whom the earth rises to speak, the air returns, the fire spreads, the water cascades to vapor, at whose first step in the woods the apperception of still pointedness tightens and is exalted, all rarity of common numbers that takes the breath away and gives it back, above and below the sight, the tree line, the fences to paradise unlinked and the children's use of just the places they do use, again and again

take the felt slight rise of unlessening
love and hammer unlost in the blood that
step cut
shared

you give

122

Arpa
que tiene en vez de cuerdas
corazones y llamas

Harp
that has instead of strings
hearts and flames

— Federico García Lorca

BOWLS

Now polish the crucible
and in the bowl distill

— H.D.

form is cut from the lute's neck, tone is from the bowl
Oak boughs alone over Selloi

— Ezra Pound

a silence in the Central Tree
the leaves gone down the autumn flood and winter frozen
barest branch click
only occasionally

who left the prints? hearing us? we missed?

sap listeners   tree leavers   bark gnawers   wind freaks

from-the-sky-who-dwells-*in*-the-tree?   "foolish to think"

«earth-bedded servants of the unsilent bowl»   "people live there"

«and with unwashen feet»

birdless, empty   and yet the great space all
                                              «packed full of ominous sound»

still
can you hear it
tell?

I saw the Mouse King last night, and thought at first, he was so big, he was a cat
preoccupied with what to do about the mice bouncing three feet in the air thick around the
    toilet
I looked at him a long long time before I saw who he was
then he turned his head, rolled a whisker, arched an eyebrow, and smiled

        we're in it together
                bay-bee

so sad rocks   so had the mantic   so dance accumulate, alveolate home deep
the lost sea   brow-laid leaf to eat   in the earth their heart listens
                                      this is their bliss, in this delight the
                                          living
                                      share in the light

great Mouse King, Apollo-My-Watcher
would have slain you if he'd known who he was looking at when he was still so pissed off at the
    myriad mice-mc-boing-boings pinning him down in the bathroom he couldn't see straight

wrath clouded granted second
    sight to recognize

so quick the rise   redemption give?

as know the tile glaze breaks under winter
    throne in that dark?

as unwitting gone into the coils of oracle's desire
     to heal?

as gnawed the sweat-soaked straps of war to found for exile
    home?

face of its own   whiskers rolled and smile own
    like of the hand up holding the head to figure out what the fuck, own
    own, the blindfold given, taken away
    own, the muscle taut to tell
    own, the like
    light, the own

[for Jonathan Williams' 50th birthday]

According to the *Vita Metrica* of his life, Pindar died in Argos at the age of 80 (probably in 438 BC). In the words of the Suda lexicon:

> His life ended as he had wished it to; in answer
> to his prayer for the finest of life's blessings, he
> met death quickly in the theater, lying in the
> arms of his beloved Theoxenus.

> [tr. Roy Arthur Swanson, *Pindar's
> Odes* (Bobbs-Merrill, 1974)]

Theoxenus came from an illustrious family of the island of Tenedos (present-day Bozcaada), South of the entrance to the Dardanelles. For his brother, Aristagoras, on his election to the ruling council or Prytaneia of the island, Pindar wrote his *Nemean* 11, and for Theoxenus this passionate encomium and declaration of love, one of his last poems (fragment 108 Bowra, 123 Snell, 131 Turyn). This version, it can't be called a translation, this paraphrase of Pindar's great condensed ode is offered with every debt acknowledged to the renderings in Swanson, in Bowra's *Pindar* (Oxford, 1964), and in Constantine Trypanis' *Penguin Book of Greek Verse* (1971) — to a poet for whom, in Whitman's words, «Bodies are all spiritual. — All words are spiritual — nothing is more spiritual than words».

My heart, we ought to pick the buds of love
when they fit our years
but whoever just catches sight of the flashes
burning out of the eyes of Theoxenus
not carried off in the breakers of desire
had his black heart hammered out of bronze and iron

in an ice fire
Unexalted by Dark-eyed Aphrodite
he drudges desperately for gold
or shameless as a hooker
flutters every street, propositioning the soul
But because of Her I am eaten by that heat

and melt like the wax of divine bees
every time I look at the fresh-fleshed youth of boys
Surely by Puget also
Seduction dwells, and Favor
has brought up the son of Edgar

our makers beside us
not the watcher, not the doer
not the union in us

        over the indented knotted tarsel, across the blue-
           laid flooring, over the checkered pavement
        passed through the three flame points to the
           rubbled hillside where the thorn bush marks
        putrefaction
        by *the others, we*
        raised by the Elephant and the Goat carried
        to the bone gripped, made
        but not our makers, beside us

    to come to, by the worst done
    on an island far in the North
    or hanging upside-down over a railing above the raging freeway, grabbed
    Victory?   Brought back up?   Penitence?
          Blinding sight?

    the dark male meat by the tall birds
            flown?

    unmade, remade   for the worst done
                    from the waist down
                    up, by the waste won

    over and over and over and over
    doubles, the doubles doubles, together through together
    and every bit of it in a tongue nobody understands, not the speakers, not the
        secret researchers, not the stoned freak loonies, no rain, no bring, no fruit,
        not one word, not first syllable dick doodah
    and still our makers, beside us, who come

last night I was weeping, lying on the floor over into the corner from under the table, to sleep, in total despair at my fucked-up life — in Grenier and his friend's chicken coop or tool shed made into house — out in the sticks — the intensity of the scene has persisted all day, no more so than when watching Disney at 6 about the kid gone to live with his great-uncle, a Pennsylvania Dutch curer, healer, *brocher*, the kid already able to send himself out into wolves', owls' bodies — and the old great-uncle told him of all our *double nature*, and the dangers of the body left then without any senses to protect it — certainly this time the *watching* self was more intent and vividly aware than ever before — but not yet the *watched*, enacting self looking back at the watcher, can that be, too, and endure? — it all came back again, at Helen's for Sunday music with the Petrees and the piano student from Lisbon, Paul — peeing during one of the breaks I could recognize the exact state of distance in the dream with Grenier and the other, was the same as in "real life", whoever the "Grenier" was — but those modes of relation are, among others, what are "kept", "come over" — innate, "willingness", is "reluctance

James C. Malin, 8 Feb 1893-26 Jan 1979

so the lodge, of history,
of sorrow

133

tears, for a lodge of sorrow, seeds, or grit for, for that long house
and smoke of memory, history's time afire

something about, we need to, wait for, the work, to finish
waiting, outside, what did we bring along, to do, waiting?

and Sue Whosername came by completely sloshed out of her mind just as we sat down with the
star, used to be the star distributor from Lay-seen, and fell right down in the booth next to us, not
knowing who the fuck we were, "well, and say, and how old *are* you?"

good trouble, out of craft, who

compassion of grave stones where

> brief sea   *know* laps *them*

[two requiem études]

«and sing in endles morn of light»

that in the secret marriage join
     as from, so soon, the sorrow cloth
     took tears, bright eyes to wear again
down hearts' red stone

*

plain sorrow lodge undraped all the long long living room and back
outside, black hatchments on the balcony
but in, bare walls to blue the tears
the salt heart sea back, listening

the Chamber of Reflection — Death
mirrors us, we mirror Death — who's
reached by the Chain of Union?
'indissoluble in their chaos' — Hunkered
and Erect Clods, Discreet and Wise
Chaos, and Chaos Disentangled

and these, our faculty of divination
futureless, but out of time telling, anyway
'I saw it come true' not really a song
or even made up while it lasts
but more ingenious yet
inexhaustible our limits to know
but still recognize when it hits

pogo sticks à Poulenc
soft as chalumeau

by the river, eagles
in the shallows, reedlets

to accumulate rites

to eventuates flower

come hybrid pollens to new season come

persistent taking of the way through the woods

feet may give   than sidewalk street

that old back pasture that it know so well

new hustle

sweet   forcing   floor

[reading Blok]

waste by use— when now what use worries the pants legs? the young poets feel, they're called to? what was it at 16, c. 1952? — another excitement *not of this place but elsewhere*, that was at the same time the hidden, former, old-yet-ever-to-show-forth *present town*, to reach to — what was to strive for was, now I'd probably say, from all I drew on then and who, *full praise* — but then, closer to *make it all up new*? — but according to recent *past* ways I'd just found out about, new to me and who I knew — sex wasn't *new*, poetry *was* — trace my blood

[Lilacs K. Kat]

for Marshall Reese

aw he took da pipe

aw it wuzza piece a pipe

aw fuzza pup

blackhead-freckled Howdy Doody punk rockers, lilac men, nail men, call suddenness sandbag sundopers certain aromatic pipe-of-dreams flow, not color, silk-seemed-to-turn-from, about-to-sing-together-to, the question might be, *make-it-(up)-with-him*? (gesturing to the right), sneak off the shirts first, check out your pockets, no p.j.'s, voiceless bilabial pendejo fricatives, all made out of unplaited horniness, splendor'd-home-to-go

a panicled head of dreams, a hit hard but not heard bed of pipes, a rhinestone ridgehead glitter-topp'd coiffure vibratory swinette heaven, plunked

uneasy the gut grip to, from, long long after

naw, nix, nothin' up yet, knucks down, dinks, but eyes, you got mine, swingin'

and the itch, yunna stan, movillis, soitenly, soitenly, of ears, e-erhs, eee-uhrs

yours, o Great Momma, yours, all yours

[soar heart overheard]

— well, he preaches a good sermon, quiet, gym rest kind of back to it, you know the sweat's been there, but he don't *smell* to

— like *to*, but not *too* close to, an *old* Dexter beat, bitten scripture boogie rumba proud, but come down *hard* from, mean?

— high noon! high noon!
  chase the silk! sip spirit! hear?

— I wouldn't used to think it was all just sway class chic, but then that knot's been hit and hit, and hit, and hit *again*, till it quivers in the pits just to feel it coming, -proud?

— and *then* the tent gets ripped open, and *then* the spears get scattered all to hell and gone and back, and election misses, and where we thought *love* was, *we* was, without it, right?

— and my head's a balloon, closer to the moon than the man in come down in, but my heart *hears* across that vacuum

— o *la*, like it *never* heard before — *mercy!* — I got drops here, when I close my eyes, and *whomp*, to prove it

— and falling for every heart, and green green grass always to come down in, and a need I never knew before, just to *be* there

— cheep, *cheep*! and someone just *too too* to help, o Lordy, help *me*, too, to get that, o *it* got that, o, "*I* remember Clifford", -beat?

143

Skodnick asks about   the Gates of Asia, the hinges
of the continent

up against the body
leaning up against the hinges, bending

quill and some oil in a cup

and the doors'll swing

whose heart?   without a squeak

ignorant oil

high school but older babble behind in the back of the bus of couples — faggot jokes, enforced card games, kids crying slapped to shut up, wifey-hubby kissy-killer blither — quietness a sign of . . . scarecrows? serious impertinence, impermanence? root pride? good rude sense of the traveller, anyway, at the same time chatter can be — but not chatter, incessant loud *yuk-yuk-fucking-yuk-yuk*, it's always got to be *insisted* it's right to enjoy, e.g., the card game turned into backgammon — gathered by the lot of the journey, how it ends up sitting together, like, not -minded, but -vibed, -chinned, congenial-congenial, jawbone for nose, instincts like accidence instruct — in Gerrit's letter: «poetic "elitism" [which grows — & can reconcile Mallarmé's (& S. George's) & Lautréamont's (poetry is for everyone) . . . & the mirror of supernatural economics» — the Montana Texas great-grand-mother finally came and picked up the 16-months-old boy of the couple across the aisle and in front, who'd been crying ever since Denver, and got him to sleep — "usually I can hypnotize a child in five minutes, he took longer than any I can remember, his little muscles were just like knots" — calling to imaginary animals in the air, "hey dogs, come on, dogs, ooo-ooo, hey, come on, hey dogs", spell weaving — what all we have in common as willingness to make out of time, and what can't be made up for, no matter *out of* or *out in* — limits to go to see the sacred places on the table with the scrambled eggs and hashbrowns, between and on — *then we stopped and waited for the signal to come on, we heard return in us*

[Reunion]

a new Law of Love   (Knight Rose Croix)

a new Lord over Love   (HD/RD)

twin crosses, scaffolds
«the arms of the cross changed into wings»

                         . . . dusty crown
   simultaneously   *dust and feathers*
                          leaves and dust

                         one-line *engines*
                         master turned and tuned

rust cut, no more just melo-, phano-, logo-, mytho-, morpho-, psycho-, but *more* —
to stand with the things of Nature already down a separate road from the things of Nature

X's in support, extensity   «so that the lines . . .
to multiply the unknown times   do not meet»

                         she opened the snake's jaws
                         with her fingers and rubbed
                         the fangs lingeringly, I just
                         used my shoe

"she's my ex-" and "she's my tension"
'*tens-hut*! said the mule joke, "first you gotta get his '*tens*hun —
now laht the fahr"

                      did Pike read Boehme?
                      out of the fire of Wrath and Civil War —

the deep pleasure, the rightness hearing the rituals done in the local common speech

                   «The fire would not warm, if it could not
                   also burn, the human flesh»

                        — Love?

                           its doctrine
                       the acme of the inquisitor

the full penalty of the obligation
losing, *never* finding the Word?

so finally «the assumption about who's there»
is the crux, and «who cannot answer»?

[pastorale]

not for a long time such a soup, the frozen carcasses of weeks of Sunday roast chickens, simmered all a Saturday afternoon, with onion and celery and parsley, thyme, basil, and California bay — slow and skimmed, on past sunset, then strained and the bones and meat set aside to cool, to pick for salad later — the stock cooked on with rice till the grains butterfly open, fat — shots of Tabasco in the bowl and chopped parsley, coarse fresh-crushed black pepper — sourdough rolls under the broiler till the crust browns almost black, flesh soft and buttered — cold jug chablis and salad, and afterwards coffee and brandy and bitter-chocolate coffee beans, creased with a dent — and the pleasure of it warmed up for lunch next day just as great, pepper and parsley and Tabasco again, and a drop of soy, with wheat crackers this time, and good cheap French vermouth on the rocks

not for a long time such a deep, muted underglow, to reflect the soul turn's own reflection back into the days, wet, dark, up-welling, mid-November

[for Ken Grenier]

his art: beyond intention made

.

«It is in his nature not to belong to any locality and not to possess any permanent abode; always he is on the road between here and yonder»

— W.F. Otto, *The Homeric Gods*

.

she made a rock — I was made? too?
    confer the birdbath flock below
        or a tallow sponge for stone for bread?
           in fact, a birdseed ball, pecked through

.

he is on the back way home, a pig sitting on a farmhouse porch playing a violin, stopping as he's looked at then starting up again, playing with the back of the Irish-harp-shaped bow, or bow held upside-down, a jig for the monument we dance around, arms and shoulders as if in habit to the music wings, *tyrants rivet feathers on the human body, the priesthood, on the human soul*, made by being interfered with in the making, pig'n'fiddle underworldly hog-heaven life, aloft — «and suddenly he joins some solitary wayfarer», and out of every earth-struck future step an ample spring leaps forth

for he is the connection maker, and he is the connection made

[homage to Nicolas Poussin]

yah I et in Arcadia ago, long long time ago, that diner used to sit right next
to Dutton's, ain't there no more, et there a lotta times, till he died, that ole
boy that run it,   Bones   Cross   even there he was, yeah, we was
pretty close back then, like George said, down there to a meeting one night
a couple of years ago, that time they come over from Missouri to visit,
looking up at all them old faded pictures of past masters on the walls, "you
know, this is a place that's known a lot of pride"

and Death says,   Even here am I
and we say back, remembering,   We, too, been

            in Arkady

The author is grateful for the opportunity to quote briefly in the text from a number of sources, including the following (translations other than those indicated are by the author):

page 3: Robert Grenier, *Oakland* (Tuumba Press, 1980), "Sunshine Line"

Thomas Meyer, *Staves Calends Legends* (The Jargon Society, 1979), «Belt & Sword / armour leap up»

Gerrit Lansing, *The Heavenly Tree Grows Downward* (North Atlantic Books, 1977), "An Inlet Of Reality, or Soul"

Virgil, *Eclogae*, V, unpublished translation by Stanley Lombardo

9: Robert Duncan, *Letters* (Jargon Books, 1958), "Preface: Signatures"

Walt Whitman, *Specimen Days*, "After Trying a Certain Book"

Sir Thomas Browne, *Hydriotaphia*, V

Lao Tzu, *Tao te ching*, 1, translated by Peter A. Boodberg, "Philological Notes on Chapter One of the *Lao Tzu*", *Harvard Journal of Asiatic Studies*, 20 (1957)

11: Gunnar Ekelöf, *Dīwān över Fursten av Emgión* (Albert Bonniers Förlag, 1965), *Dīwān*, 19

17: Gérard de Nerval, *Voyage en Orient*, "Les nuits de Ramadan", III, vi

31: Rainer Maria Rilke, *Briefwechsel Rainer Maria Rilke und Marie von Thurn und Taxis* (Niehaus & Rokitansky Verlag and Insel-Verlag, 1951), I, #138, letter of 12 Dec 1912

47: Gérard de Nerval, *Chimères*, "Vers dorés", translated by Robert Duncan, *Bending the Bow* (New Directions Books, 1968), *The Chimeras of Gérard de Nerval*, "Golden Lines"

Harry Martinson, *Passad* (Albert Bonniers Förlag, 1945), "Gudinnan av Hyn"

51: Robert Duncan, *Poems 1948-1949* (Berkeley Miscellany Editions, 1949), *The Venice Poem*, "Imaginary Instructions"

59: Osip Mandelstam, *Sobranie Sochinenii*, II (Inter-Language Library Associates, 1966), "Razgovor o Dante", II

63: Edward Dorn, *Gunslinger: Book III* (Frontier Press, 1972), "The LAWG of the Winterbook"

79: Joel Chandler Harris, *Uncle Remus*, XV, as cited in *The Century Dictionary*, "study"

Walter Benjamin, *Gesammelte Schriften*, II, 1 (Suhrkamp Verlag, 1977), "Über die Sprache überhaupt und über die Sprache des Menschen"

| page | 97: | Louis Zukofsky, *Anew* (The Press of James A. Decker, 1946), 4; *"A" 1-12* (Origin Press, 1959), 12 |

103: Federico García Lorca, *Obras completas* (Aguilar, 1974), I, "Thamar y Amnón"

109: Johannes Bobrowski, *Wetterzeichen* (Union Verlag, 1966), "An Klopstock"

114: Walt Whitman, *Leaves of Grass*, "Song of Myself", 49

116: Henry Vaughan, *Silex Scintillans, I*, "Sure, there's a Tye of Bodyes! and as they"

123: Federico García Lorca, *Obras Completas* (Aguilar, 1974), I, "[A las poesías completas de Antonio Machado]"

127: H. D., *Tribute to the Angels* (Oxford University Press, 1945), VIII

Ezra Pound, *Thrones* (New Directions Books, 1959), Canto 109

131: Roy Arthur Swanson, *Pindar's Odes* (The Bobbs-Merrill Company, 1974), commentary on Nemean 11

Walt Whitman, *An American Primer*

133: Cicero, *De divinatione*, I, 1

136: John Milton, *Poems*, "At a solemn Musick"

148: Walter F. Otto, *The Homeric Gods*, translated by Moses Hadas (Pantheon Books, 1954), III, "Olympian Deities", *Hermes*, 7